The Lesson of Moogoo-Maagooville

Karen Jensen

Illustrations by George Ostroushko

1997
Weasel Books
PO Box 460, Lakeville, Minnesota 55044–0460

First Edition
First Printing, 1997

Library of Congress Cataloging-in-Publication Data

Jensen, Karen.
    The lesson of Moogoo-Maagooville / Karen Jensen. — 1st ed.
        p.   cm.
    Summary: The friendship of Zak and Laroy helps unite Moogoo
and Maagoo, rival towns split by a bitter feud over the juice factory
they share.
    ISBN 1–880090–49–X
    [1. Vendetta—Fiction.   2. Prejudices—Fiction.   3. Stories in
rhyme.]   I. Title.
PZ8.3.J422Le   1997
[Fic]—dc21   97–15739
                                                          CIP
                                                          AC

Weasel Books are published by:
Galde Press, Inc.
PO Box 460
Lakeville, Minnesota 55044

Dedication

Mom and Dad, who taught me—
Zak and Tina, who believed in me—
Bobby J., who taught me to believe in myself—
Sarah, who kept asking me to read it again.

Always with love,
Karen

It was a Moogoo-Maagooville sort of
   morning
In May
And two Moogoo-Maagoo
   grandchoos
Were with grandpoo that day.
They were walking the town,
Seeing sights,
Having fun,
Cause Grandpoo played games
That everyone won.
They were crossing Town Square,
Sipping Moogoo-Maagoo Juice,
When there it was,
Before them,
rising up huge.
They'd seen it from far off
But never up close.
Now, here they were
Very near,
And they froze.
"Oh, Grandpoo, this statue.
I've never quite seen
Something so big and so large
Wherever I've been!"
"This statue was built to remind us,
   my dears,
How Moogoo-Maagooville was
   founded
Right here."

"Oh, Grandpoo, do tell
How this place came to be.
You were there. You can tell us
Of our history."
"Oh, Grandpoo, do tell us."
"Oh, Grandpoo, oh, please."

"All right. I will tell you.
Come sit on my knees."
So they sat and they listened
To Grandpoo's old tale
Of how Moogoo-Maagooville
Had once almost failed.

"The ones without hearts
Are the ones we should fear.
Our differences we should
Celebrate and always hold dear.
Respect one another.
It's what we must do
Work together in peace,
For the future.
For the choodroos."

You see Moogoo-Maagooville
Was once cut in two.
There was Moogoo and Maagoo
Two towns with one feud.

The town's people were different
And on sight you could see
There was trouble a-brewing
A big mess it would be.
There was Moogoo on one side
And Maagoo on the other.
And the Maas and the Moos
Were upset with each other.
The tall Maagoos had purple hair
And were referred to as Meanies.
Moogoos were short and were called curly
    haired Greenies.
They looked very different
As different could be.
And Maas thought they were better
And said so with glee.
"After all, we are taller.
Our hair is purple, you see.
That states very clearly
Our brains are bigger than thees."
Now both towns grew fruit
One melons
One berries.
And together they mushed them
And made juice that was very
Yes, very oh, very good for them all.
It kept Moos very curly
And Maas very tall.
And healthy, oh, healthy
As healthy could be.
So Maas needed melons and
Moos the berries.

This is where the trouble
Really began.
The Maas refused to hear
Any Moo alternative plan.
So they argued and argued.
Both by day and by night.
The Maas thinking Moos wrong.
The Moos insisting they were right.
They argued so much
The issues got blurred.

They argued so loud
Neither side could be heard.
And that's how it went
For quite a long time.
The Moos and the Maas ignoring the signs
That their quaint little towns were about ready to fall
Because no one
No
No one
Agreed on anything at all.

There was a factory that was
    centered
Between both the towns,
Which were divided by crevasses
That went way way way down.
The factory was hooked to the towns
By two spans
That were made of big rocks pushed
    together,
The cracks filled with sand.
One was for Maas
To bring in their berries.
The other for Moos
For their melons to carry.
The juice it was made
At this factory by day
But at night, they went home,
Each their own way.
Well, the Moogoos were feeling
Just a little oppressed.
There was tension and anger
And oh, so much stress.
For the Moos got paid less
For their red melons like cherries
And worked longer to squeeze them
Together with Maa berries.
Their hourly wage was
Less than the Maas,
Who, by the way, ran the factory
They ruled.
Maas were boss.
So the Moos they expressed

That they wanted a change.
But the Maas said, "You're crazy!"
And became quite enraged.
"We were here first!
We are tall. We make more."
Said the Moos, " I don't get it,
How come and what for?
Together we grow them.

Together we squeeze.
So why are you paid more?
Tell us that, would you, please?"
"Because we are Maagoos.
We are smarter than thee.
Just be thankful you get what
    you get.
Now, back to work, squeeze!"

Now right in the middle
Of all this to-do,
There was a great friendship growing
between two choodroos.
Of course, one was a Maa
And one was a Moo.
But it just didn't matter
To these two choodroos.
There was Zak, the tall Maa
And Laroy, the Moo.
They laughed and they played as most choodroos do.
It didn't matter to them
If one was short or one tall,
They were just two choodroos playing.
That was it.
That was all.
They would meet in the morning
And romp through the day
While their poos were at work
Arguing away.
They would pretend they were grown up
And ran both the towns
And you had to be happy.
No one could frown.
"Oh, wouldn't it be great?"
Said Laroy with a grin.
"Now that would be cool!"
Said Zak, his tall friend.
"We are pals. We are buddies!
And those are the facts.
Together forever
Is our motto.
That is our pact!"

But back at the factory
Things were heating up
    fast.
Too much had been said.
Their fate had been cast.
The Maas and the Moos
Were at each other's
    throats.
Each one trying to get
The other one's goat.
And then it was said
By one very mad Moo,
"We don't need you at all!
We can do without you!"
The Maas looked at each
    other
Then replied with a smile,
"But it is our berries that
Make this juice so very
    worthwhile.
Without them you're
    nothing.
Without them you're lost.

Can you really afford
Such a terrible cost?"
"It's our melons that you
    need,"
Said the Moos with
    disgust.
"Without them this juice
Is a wipeout, a bust!"
"Oh, yeah?"
"Yeah, you heard us.
And we mean what we say.
Our melons are ours
And that's the way it will
    stay!"
"You keep them. Who
    needs them.
Our berries will do.
And don't ever think
Of coming to Maagoo."
"You stay far from Moogoo
If you know what is best!
You keep to the east
And we'll take the west."

And with that they all left
For their two separate towns.
For the first time ever
The factory shut down.
It was quiet and empty.
There was not a sound.
Just an eerie silence
Echoing around.
Now back at the borders
Of both of the towns,
Crowds began gathering
Word had gotten around
That melons and berries
Would no longer be shared,
And if someone tried stealing
They'd better beware.
Both populations said
Guards would be placed
At the entrance of each town
Just to be safe.
In Moogoo and Maagoo
No one could think straight.
There was panic and fear
Laced with anger and hate. zq
"Post the guards! Watch our melons!
We must keep the Maas out!
Protect what is ours!"
Became the Moogoo town shout.
And the Maas weren't much better
In their quest to be right,
"To survive Moos need berries.
When they come for them, we'll fight."

GREENIES KEEP OUT

11

Meanwhile, Laroy and Zak
Knew nothing at all
Of the mess that had happened
As they had played ball.
The sun in the sky was beginning to set.
Zak said, "Gotta go. See ya."
Laroy called back, "You bet!"
An early evening haze
Had settled all around
As Laroy and Zak
Jogged back to their towns.
And as sounds of feet running
Filled Maa and Moo ears
The worst of worst happened
Due to all of their fears.
"I hear them!"
"They're coming!"
"Quick, remove the main block!"
"We must keep them out!"
"Hurry! Destroy the walk!"
And with a heave and a ho
The rocks fell with a thump.
Then Zak and Laroy saw
That they needed to jump.
Jump for their lives.
Jump as far as they could.
They didn't know why
They just knew that they should.

When they had landed
They stood up a bit dazed
And saw what had happened
Through the dust and the haze.
The two highways that connected
The factory to the towns
Were gone in an instant.
They'd knocked them right down.
"Do you see what you've done?"
Said Laroy to the Moos.
"Good grief!" said Zak.
"Now what will we do?"
"We have our berries
And with them we'll make do.
We don't need Moo melons
To help see us through."

And the Moos said to Laroy,
"We are finally apart.
This is the way things should have been
From the start."
With that everyone turned
And headed for home,
Leaving Zak and Laroy
Standing alone.
In two separate towns
Divided by a distance so wide.
Laroy and Zak felt nothing
But sadness inside.
They both walked to where
There had once been a street
And the two of them wondered
If they would ever again meet.
"Remember, we are pals…"
"We are buddies. Remember our pact."
"Oh, Laroy, please, remember…"
"Don't forget me, Zak."
Now, you might think this tale over,
That the fight had been fought.
But the lesson of Moogoo-Maagooville
Was just beginning to be taught.

High in the sky
Way out in space,
The Council of Light
Had come to this place.
Where pride and greed
Had divided two towns.
Where self-destruction was coming.
It could already be found.
The two towns were fading.
It was happening quite fast.
How could they survive?
How would they last?
These were the questions
The Council must ask.
But to supply answers
Was not their task.
The answers must come
From the folks down below.
The answers that could save them
They should already have known.
So the Council of Light
Gathered way up in the sky,
For the first time ever
In one place at one time.

But things down below
Have never been quite so bad.
The Council was burdened.
The Council was sad.
There was a mother named Mary
And Carpenter Joe.
They were the first to arrive
Of this Council that glowed.
And a man called Elijah
And a father and son,

And Allah and Buddha.
They also would come.
And many more came
To light up the night.
They would work through this together
Trying to make this wrong right.
Now the last to arrive
Was a small little light.
It was the one they called Self.
It was tiny but bright.

So they all came together
And merged into one.
This emergency meeting
Of light had begun.
"Perhaps we have failed them.
Perhaps we were wrong.
Thinking that Moos and Maas
Could all get along."
"No, it is their pride that has failed them.
We have always been there.
They just didn't hear us.
They chose not to care.
We always have shown them
How it should be.
Again the choice is theirs.
They have to see.
Our message—the answer
Is easy enough.
They were put here quite simply
To love and be loved.
We can't stop this nonsense
Of who gets to be right.
They have to see
They too have the power of light.
And until they see that
There is nothing to do
But wait and to be here
And hope they pull through."
So the Council remained there
Floating way out in space,
Hoping and believing in this
Moo and Maa race.

Back in the towns
Things were not looking good.
Nothing had worked out
As they thought it would.
The factory was crumbling
And falling away.
Once a symbol of progress
It was now in a state of decay
There was no way to go
And make the repairs.
They had destroyed the roads.
Now nothing was there.
Except deep empty spaces
On either side.
Too deep to crawl down,
To jump them—too wide.
There was so much work
That seemed to never get done.
And there was no time for laughter,
No time for fun.

Whispers and murmurs
That maybe mistakes had been made
Were beginning to surface,
Hope slowly to fade.
Now the Moos' color was fading
And they were growing quite fast.
They weren't the same Moos
They had been in the past.
And the Maas, they were shrinking
A little each day.
Maas weren't the same either,
But no one would say
That maybe, just maybe
They all had been wrong.
That would mean weakness
And they must appear strong.
The towns themselves
Were crumbling from within.
There was sickness and illness
Where health had once been.
But it was the Maa and Moo choodroos
Who were paying the cost.
They were the sickest.
To them, the future was lost.

To the edge of Moogoo
Laroy went every day.
Hoping to see
If his friend Zak was okay.
And Zak made the same trip
On his side of Maagoo
Hoping Laroy was well
In his town of Moogoo.
And they shared the same thoughts
On these trips every day—
If this feud continued
The choodroos would all die away.
The choodroos couldn't make it
Without Moo and Maa juice.

But the grown poos wouldn't listen.
They had all just refused.
Laroy and Zak had
Both tried to plea,
"Look at the young ones,
Look, and you'll see."
"Look at our town.
Just look around.
Look at our lives
They've been turned upside down."
"You're only a choodroo
And this is a grown poo affair."
That was the end of discussion.
It seemed they just didn't care.

Now way up above
Way high in the sky,
One Light of the Council
Was about ready to fly.
"Oh, I can't take this.
They'll never figure this out!"
"Now Self, just calm down.
Don't get lost in your doubts.

We will not desert them.
This is where we must be.
Now, shhh…look and listen.
There are two
Who have seen."

Laroy and Zak
Were about ready to bust.
If the grown poos didn't care
They had to, they must.
So Laroy breathed in
And yelled the loudest he could,
"Zaaaak! Can you hear me?"
How he hoped that he would.
And at the same time,
Zak had yelled too.
"Laroy! Please hear me.
Please, please, please do!"
Well, their voices collided
And bounced all around.
Echoing first up
And then all the way down.
Then the voices rose up
To the ears of each friend.
They both jumped with excitement,
Not feeling the tremors begin.
"Laroy, listen, things are awful.
I don't know what to do.
We need Moo melons
Or we Maas, we are through."
"And we need Maa berries
Or we'll be right alongside,
Why are grown poos so stubborn?
Do we all have to die?"
"Don't give up Laroy.
There must be a way.
Remember our pact.
Friends forever we'll stay."

But before a plan could be made
For stopping this waste
The two towns started shaking
All over the place.
Yes, the ground was shaking
And the factory was too.
Zak and Laroy couldn't think
What to do.
Then the factory began falling
Spewing rocks in the air
And sand it went flying
Covering things everywhere.
Zak and Laroy
Were both thrown and knocked down.
They were caught in this hailstorm
Of rock hitting the ground.
Both of them thought
That the end had now come.
It was the grown poos who did this!
How stupid! How dumb!
To think that this place
Was too small for them all.
Was it really so important
Who was short or who tall?

And just as it started
It stopped just like that.
And the place where the factory
Had been, now was flat.
Now there was no space
That divided these friends.
The factory had fallen
And filled it all in.
Well Zak and Laroy now knew
What to do.
The end that was coming
Was the end of this feud.
Up they both leaped
And started to carry
Melons one way
The other way berries.

But the poos from each town
Started pushing them back.
They had all come to see
What the shaking had done
And what they saw shocked them.
Now their two towns were one.
And the Maas wouldn't let
Laroy come in.
And the Moos pushed Zak back
Back to back with his friend.
There they were stopped
Both holding the fruits.
Laroy faced Maas.
Zak looked at the Moos.

There they all stood
A standoff at best.
Then those brave choodroos
Put their faith to the test.
Their faith in each other.
Their faith in poo kind.
"Excuse me," they both said.
"Please move. Would you mind?"
"You seem to forget," said the grown poos,
"Yes, we mind.
Now get out of here. Leave.
We don't mix with your kind!"
Then Zak yelled, "Stop! Stop it!
Just let it end."
"And who are you?" the Moos said.
Laroy said, "He's my friend."

The silence that followed
Stopped both Maas and Moos.
What was going on
Between these young choodroos?
They stood for what seemed like
Hours and stared
At Zak and Laroy
This odd little pair.
Then one shrinking Maa said,
"How can this be?"
And one of the Moos said,
"Tell us, what is the fee?
For this fruit that he brings
To our town of Moogoo?
Come on, tell us.
What's in it for you?"

And Zak said, "Nothing.
They are free. There's no cost.
We just want our future
That you grown poos have lost.
For in your battle for power
There's been no winner, no gain.
And in your fight to be different
We all look the same."
Then Laroy spoke out,
"Look, we are fading real fast
And if you don't let us through
All we'll have is our past."
The Maas looked at the Moos
And the Moos looked at the Maas

And they saw for the first time
The root of their flaws.
Then a light went on
Inside Maa and Moo heads
And quite clearly they saw
Where their actions had led.
What made them different was now
    fading.
What was special was gone.
How had this started?
How had they gone wrong?
And after all of this time
They listened with their hearts.
And slowly, one by one,

The crowds on both sides moved
    apart.
They not only parted
But two lines had spread out.
And they began passing
Their fruit all about.
They worked through the day
And into the night,
Making Moogoo-Maagoo juice,
Making things right.
They made plans to rebuild
And make the towns one.
The founding of Moogoo-Maagooville
At last had begun.

The Moos and the Maas
Arrived at peace on that night.
Even the sky was alive
With lights that shined bright.
Yes, way up in the sky,
Way up above,
The Council of Light
Was aglow with unconditional love.
And Laroy smiled
At his very tall friend.
And Zak winked at Laroy
And they said with a grin,

"We are pals. We are buddies.
Those are the facts!
Together forever!
That's our motto.
That is our pact."
And the council adjourned.
From their meeting of light.
But they'd always remain
Through the darkest of nights,
Hoping and loving
To the light of each day.
That is what they do.
That's just their way.

"And that is the story
Of why we are here.
Remember it, grandchoos,
Never forget it, my dears."
"Grandpoo, is the statue
Of Laroy and Zak?"
"Yes it is, grandchoos,
And that is a fact."
"Whatever happened to
Laroy and Zak?"
"They grew up and had families.
Now come on, it's time to head back."

As they walked past
The statue in the town square,
Grandpoo read the plaque
At the base of the pair.
"The ones without hearts
Are the ones we should fear.
Our differences we should
Celebrate and always hold dear.
Respect one another.
It's what we must do.
Work together in peace,
For the future.
For the choodroos."

As his grandchoos skipped ahead
Singing a song,
Grandpoo saw his old friend
Herding his own grandchoos along.
"Well, hello Laroy."
"How are you Zak?"
They shook hands
And patted each other on the back.
"We still on for Melonberry Tea?"
"Wouldn't miss it." Zak said.

"Then I'll see you at three."
Zak moved on watching
His old friend the Moogoo,
Romping and playing
As grandpoos do with grandchoos.
And Zak knew very soon
Laroy would be telling the tale
Of how Moogoo-Maagooville
Had once almost failed.

To order additional copies of this book, please send full amount plus $4.00 for postage and handling.

Send orders to:

GALDE PRESS, INC.
PO Box 460
Lakeville, Minnesota 55044

Credit card orders call 1–800–777–3454

Write for free catalog!